Our WORLD is WHOLE

Written by GAIL BUSH ★ Illustrated by JENNIE POH

This world, our world,
is whole.
Every day.

When we believe it to be so.

Uncle Harry believes that
my birthday card is always late
because

he sends it from Providence on a
turtle's back,

slow and steady,
late belated.

Uncle Harry has never met our neighbor
Mrs. Turner but…

Mrs. Turner believes that
she likes grocery shopping
because

there is a rhythm to the aisles,
milk and yogurt, this and that,

lettuce, carrots, chitchat.

Mrs. Turner does not know Jerry, our cousin from California but...

Jerry believes that
you cannot cook too much food
because

too many tamales would not be enough,

masa y masa,

más masa.

Jerry has met ObiCat but she does not really know him...

Obi believes that
people open books
because

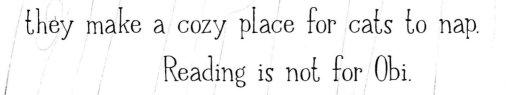

they make a cozy place for cats to nap.
Reading is not for Obi.

Napping is for Obi,
     purr and stretch,
          yawn snooze.

ObiCat has known Dad all of his nine lives...
Dad believes that
baseball has been very good to him.
He is a grown man but
because

Dad plays baseball,
Mom says that
he is still a boy of summer,

run sun,

hit it down, Daddy.

Dad knows his biggest fan.

Mom believes that
it is the pull of family
that makes the whole world go around.

Yes, the sun shines, the moon orbits, and stars
twinkle but
because

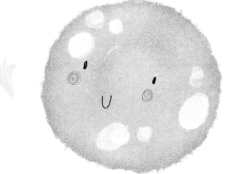

families spin together
the world is whole,
to the sun and the moon and the stars

and
back again.

I believe in
  Uncle Harry,
    Mrs. Turner,
      Cousin Jerry,
        and ObiCat,

and Dad and Mom because

all together
we are we,

late belated,

chitchat,

más masa,

moon stars.

run sun,

yawn snooze,

And they all believe that
I am part
of
our whole world

just
because
I
am
me.

For My Minnow Moms
Claire, Josette, Hannah, Laura & Meredith
–Gail

For Jasmine and Esme
–Jennie

SLEEPING BEAR PRESS™

2395 South Huron Parkway, Suite 200
Ann Arbor, MI 48104
www.sleepingbearpress.com

Printed and bound in the United States.

10 9 8 7 6 5 4 3 2 1

Library of Congress Cataloging-in-Publication Data

Names: Bush, Gail, author. | Poh, Jennie, illustrator.
Title: Our world is whole / by Gail Bush ; illustrated by Jennie Poh.
Description: Ann Arbor, Michigan : Sleeping Bear Press, [2020] |
Audience: Ages 4-8. | Summary: Illustrations and rhythmic text affirm a
young girl's belief that everyone in the world is connected, from relatives
far and near, to her chatty neighbor, to her family cat, to herself.
Identifiers: LCCN 2019047092 | ISBN 9781534110274 (hardcover)
Subjects: CYAC: Belonging (Social psychology)–Fiction.
| Mindfulness (Psychology)–Fiction.
Classification: LCC PZ7.1.B88766 Our 2020 | DDC [E]–dc23
LC record available at https://lccn.loc.gov/2019047092